Morgan's Boat Ride

By **Hugh MacDonald**

Illustrated by **Anna Bald**

The Acorn Press
Charlottetown
2014

ACORNPRESS

P.O. Box 22024
Charlottetown, Prince Edward Island
C1A 9J2
acornpresscanada.com

Printed in China
Edited by Sherie Hodds
Designed by Matt Reid

Library and Archives Canada Cataloguing in Publication

MacDonald, Hugh, 1945-, author
Morgan's boat ride / written by Hugh MacDonald ; art
by Anna Bald.

ISBN 978-1-894838-96-2 (pbk.)

I. Bald, Anna, illustrator II. Title.

PS8575.D6306M67 2014   jC813'.54   C2014-901086-9

Canada

Canada Council   Conseil des Arts
for the Arts   du Canada

The publisher acknowledges the support of the Government of Canada
through the Canada Book Fund of the Department of Canadian Heritage for
our publishing activities. We also acknowledge the support of the Canada
Council for the Arts for our publishing program.

To our amazing grandchildren: Zahra, Alexander, Vaughan, Ruca, Emerson, Emma, Grace and Della.

—H.M.

For Sue Hinton and Andrew Bald

—A.B.

Morgan ran bare toes through the cool grass under the tall birches beside the riverbank.

She knew she shouldn't swim in the river when her mother wasn't there. She climbed inside the little boat and just imagined she was floating in the big water.

She dipped her toes in the pool of warm water in the
bottom of the boat and admired the white gulls in the
blue sky overhead. She didn't notice the tide slowly
rising and the boat drifting away from the shore.

In the cottage, Morgan's mommy heard
the television in the front room.

"Mommy's almost done," she called out to Morgan.
"We'll go out and play real soon, dear."

Morgan had already noticed that the boat was
drifting down the river. She and Skipper were
having fun. The sun was warm on her shoulders
and the water in the boat was lovely to sit in. All
around her the world felt new and interesting.

She watched Mr. Turner dig in the red sand with a big fork. Mrs. Turner knelt beside him holding a metal bucket. She picked white clams from the sand, rinsed them in the water and dropped them in the bucket.

"Hi," yelled Morgan. "We're sailing."

Mrs. Turner jumped to her feet and looked out at the passing boat. She and Mr. Turner began to shout and wave their arms.

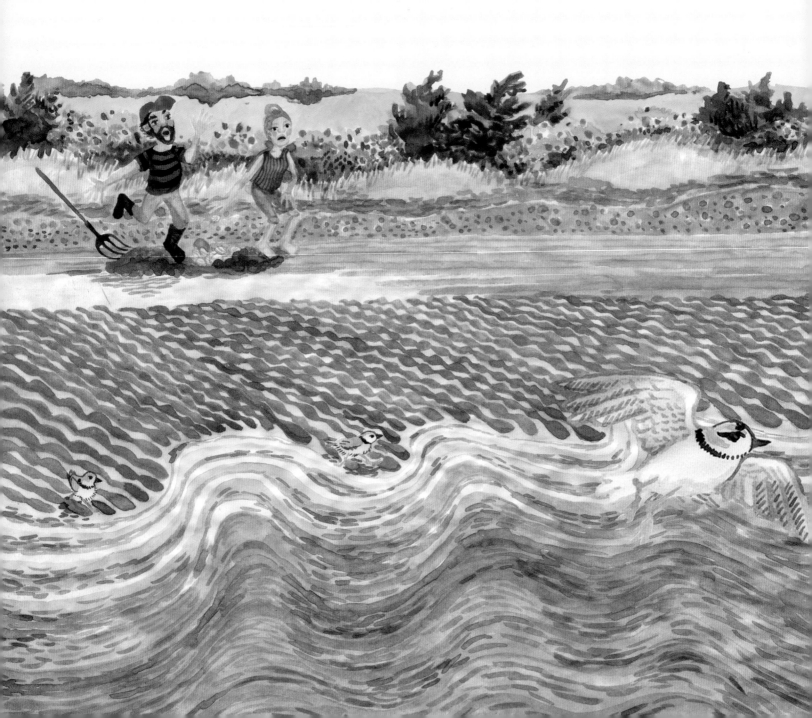

But the current was strong and the boat moved fast. Morgan and Skipper were past the Turners already and couldn't hear what they were saying. There was even more water in the boat now. She giggled and kicked her legs. She could make it splash very high.

They floated past Mr. Taweel, who stood in water halfway up the sides of his hip waders. He was fishing for trout near where the creek emptied into the river.

"Hi there, Mr. Taweel," Morgan shouted.

Mr. Taweel was so surprised to see them that his funny hat with the feathers and hooks fell in the water. He called Morgan's name, but she was too far past him to hear.

GUPPY

From up ahead Morgan heard children's voices carried back to her on the steady breeze. She watched children jumping off a small wooden raft into the river. As Morgan's boat approached, one of the big kids yelled and pointed. The children on the raft began to wave their arms and shout.

"Hi there, big kids," Morgan yelled.
"Look at us, we're sailing."

She tried to hear what the kids were saying, but they were calling out all at once and she couldn't make out a word.

For a short while there were no more people to see.

Morgan saw big fluffy clouds when she looked up and big fluffy clouds when she looked down. She laughed as birds splashed their wings against the water. The current carried her towards the mouth of the river.

She saw a sailboat up ahead. Morgan liked sailboats.

"Hello, sailboat!" she shouted.

A head popped up, just as a great gust of wind caught the tall sail. Morgan laughed as head and feet and everything in between fell into the river. The sailor waved his arms wildly in the air and shouted something Morgan couldn't hear.

The little rowboat moved out into the harbour. Morgan stopped splashing and Skipper began to bark. They looked up at a large hull as it slowed to a stop and loomed over them. The boat was so tall that for a moment they couldn't see the sky.

"Hello, big boat!" she yelled, and Skipper danced
about and barked. Morgan began to laugh.

"Hello little girl and little dog!" shouted a tall woman
in a huge pair of coveralls. "I'm coming down to get
you both. Don't stand up."

When they arrived on board the big boat, Morgan
smiled at the people who were standing there.

"Hi there, people in the big boat. Did you see us in
our little boat? We floated down the river to here."

Morgan watched the shore as the big boat sailed back up the river. They passed the place where the sailboat had tipped, passed the raft, passed the spot where Mr. Taweel had stood fishing, and passed the sand where the Turners had been digging for clams. Everyone was gone.

As they approached the cottage, Skipper began to bark
again, and Morgan said, "We're home! Can we get off now?"

"Your mother is waiting for us at the wharf in town,"
said the sailor. "So you and Skipper can enjoy the trip."

As they travelled, Morgan waved at people
along the shore and they waved back.

Finally, they arrived at the wharf. Morgan looked at all the people waiting and said, "Hi, everyone. We're home from our trip. I sailed down the river with Skipper in our little boat. We sailed up the river in this big boat. I'm hungry. Is there something to eat?"

Everyone laughed and her mother blew her
nose into a big handkerchief.

"Morgan's mother hugged her
very tightly. "Mommy's sorry,
Morgan. Were you scared?"

Morgan laughed, "No, Mommy. I played
in our boat and talked to people on the
river. I had fun watching the world go by."